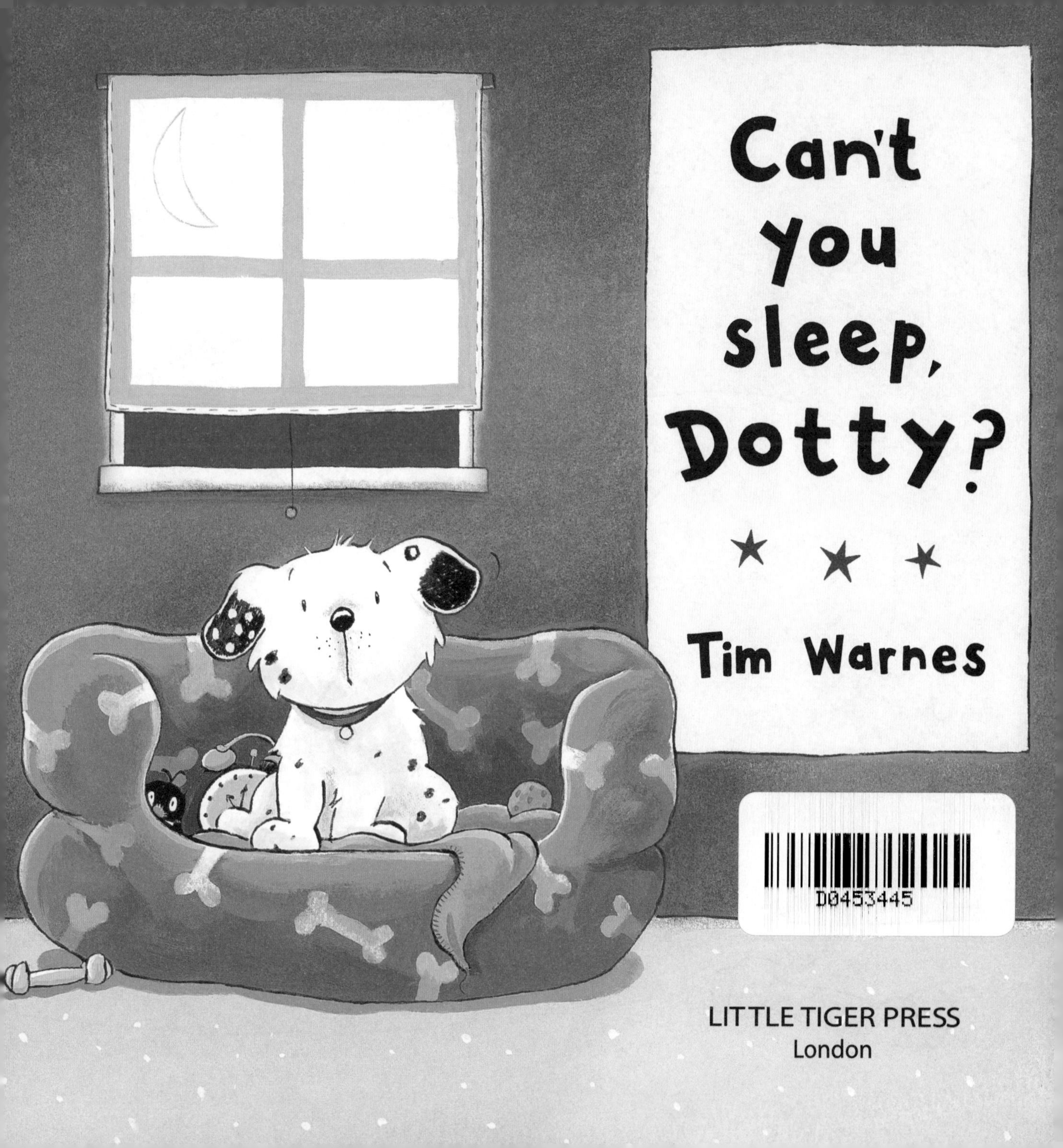
Can't you sleep, Dotty?
Tim Warnes
D0453445
LITTLE TIGER PRESS
London

Tick! Tick!

Dotty couldn't sleep.
It was her first night
in her new home.

She tried sleeping upside down. She even tried lying on the floor.

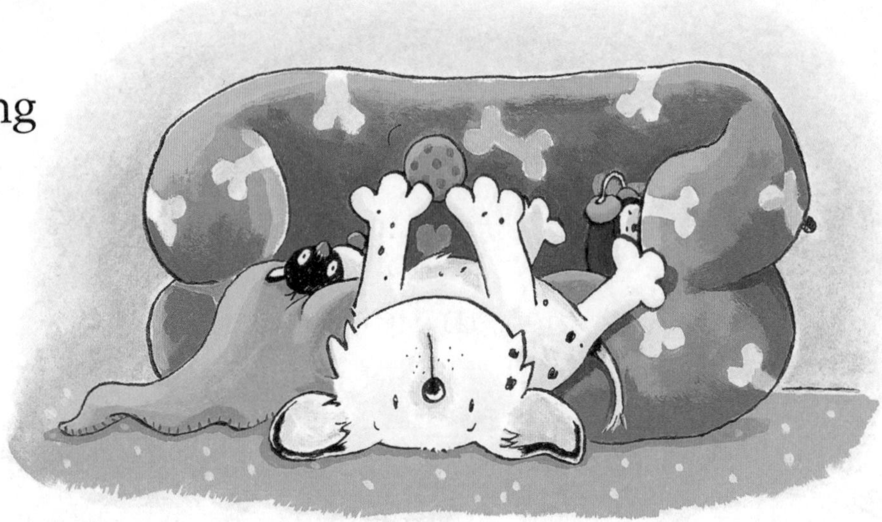

AWOOOOOOOOOOOOO

But still Dotty couldn't sleep.

Dotty's howling woke up Pip the mouse.

"Can't you sleep, Dotty?" he asked. "Perhaps you should try counting the stars."

But Dotty could only count up to one. *That* wasn't enough to send her to sleep.

What could she do next?

AWOOOOOOOOO

Susie the bird was awake now. "Can't you sleep, Dotty?" she twittered. "I always have a little drink before I go to bed."

Dotty went to her bowl and
had a little drink.

But then she made
a little puddle.
Well *that*
didn't help!
What *could* Dotty
do to get to sleep?

Whiskers the rabbit had woken up, too. "Can't you sleep, Dotty?" he mumbled sleepily. "I hide away in my burrow at bedtime. That always works."

Wag!
Wag!

Dotty dived under her blanket so that only her bottom was showing. But it was all dark under there with no light at all.

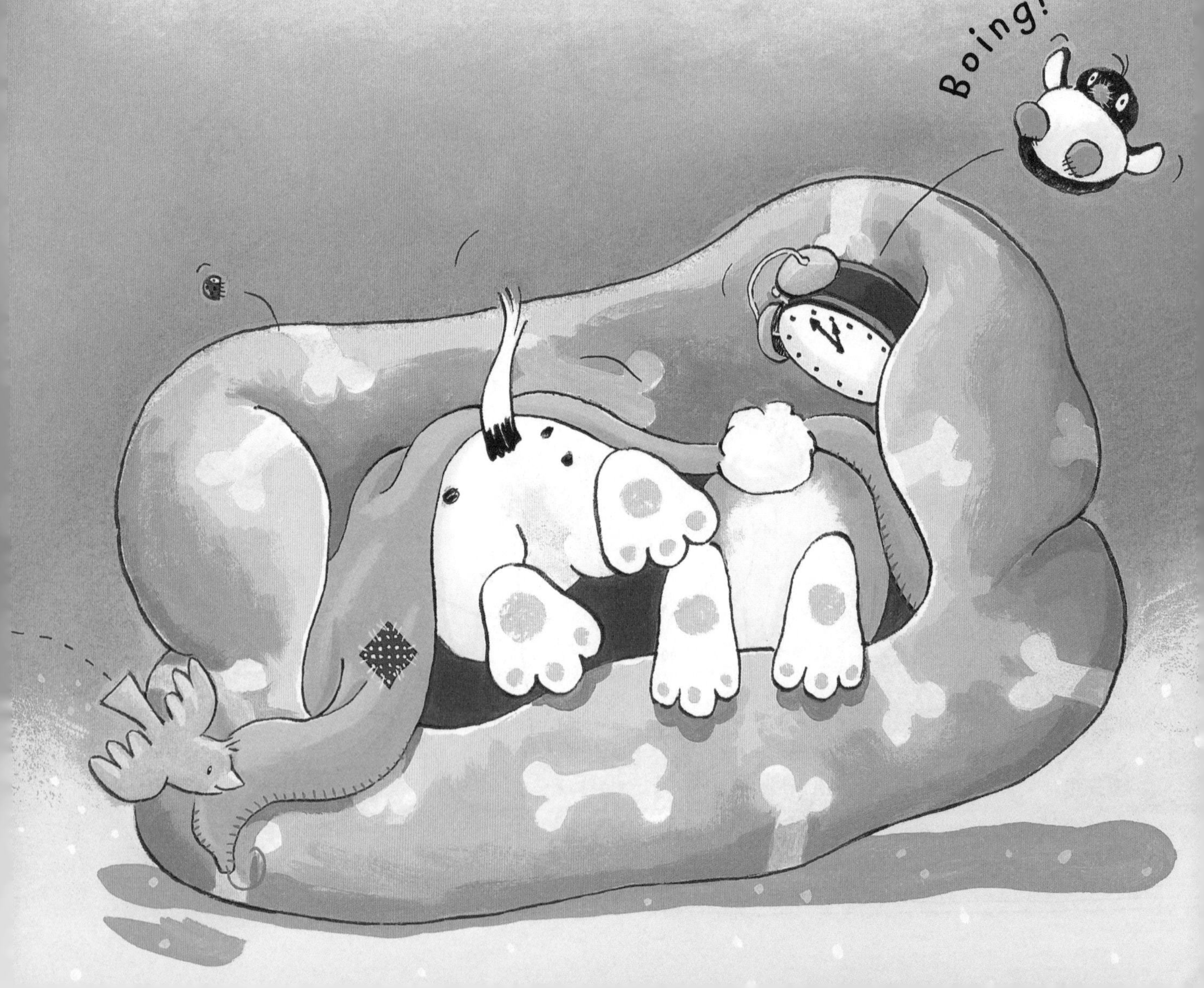

Dotty was too scared to go to sleep.

Tommy the tortoise
poked his head from
out of his shell.

"Can't you sleep, Dotty?" he sighed. "I like to sleep where it's bright and sunny."

Dotty liked that idea . . .

. . . and turned on her torch!

ZZZZZZZZZZZZ

For Noah x

LITTLE TIGER PRESS
1 The Coda Centre, 189 Munster Road,
London SW6 6AW
www.littletiger.co.uk

First published in Great Britain 2001
This edition published 2012

Visit Tim Warnes at
www.ChapmanandWarnes.com

Printed in China • LTP/1800/0794/0913
4 6 8 10 9 7 5 3

"Turn it off, Dotty!"
shouted all her friends.
"*We* can't get to sleep now!"

Poor Dotty was too
tired to try anything else.
Then Tommy had a great idea . . .

he helped Dotty into her bed.
What Dotty needed for the first
night in her new home was . . .

. . . to snuggle up among
all her new friends. Soon
they were all fast asleep.
Night-night, Dotty.

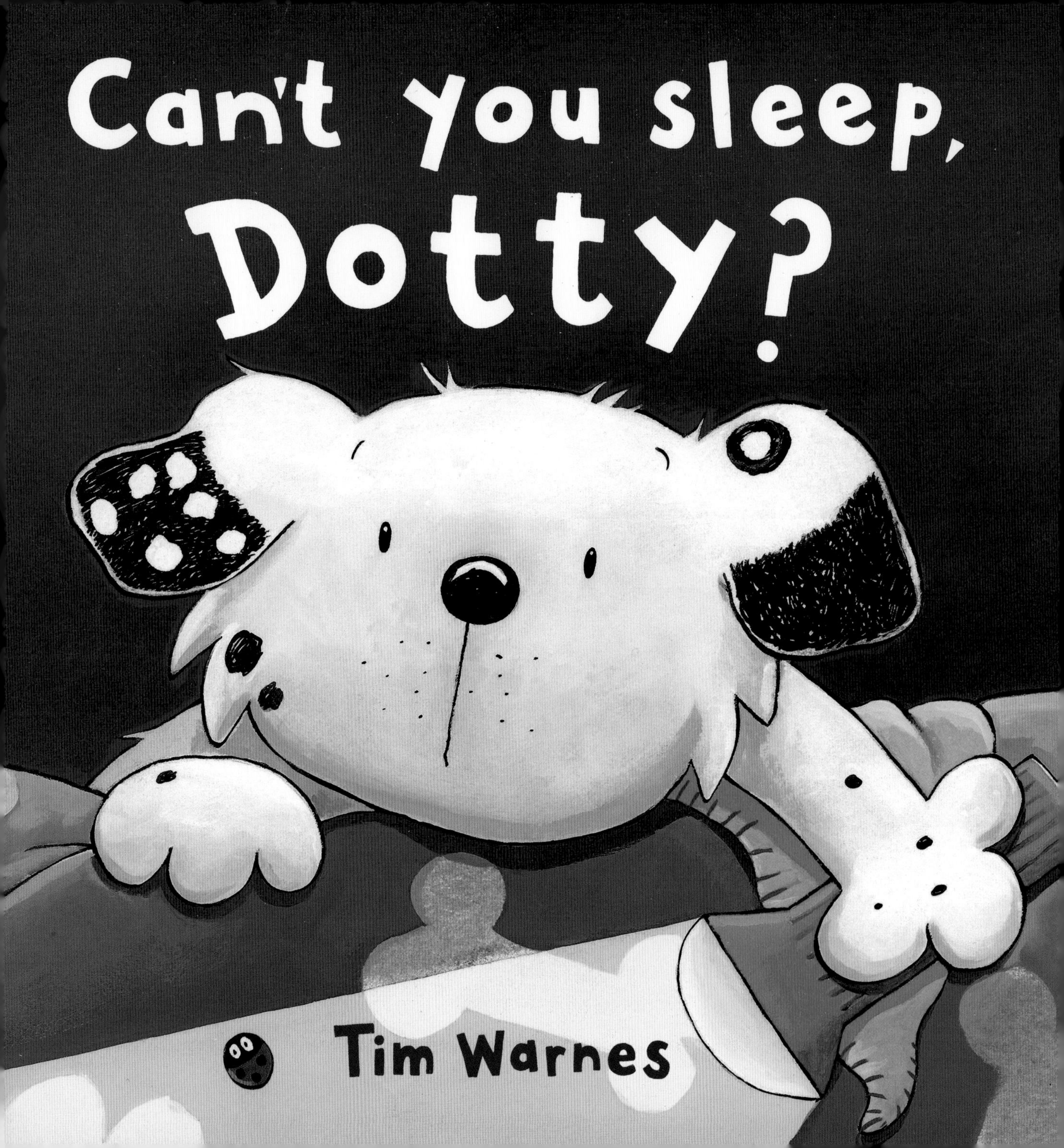
Can't you sleep,
Dotty?
Tim Warnes